Joy Cowley & Giselle Clarkson

THE TINY WOMAN'S COAT

GECKO PRESS

The tiny woman wanted a coat.

"Where will I get the cloth?"

"You can have our leaves,"
said the autumn trees.
Rustle, rustle, rustle.

The tiny woman wanted a coat.

"Where will I get some scissors?"

"Try me instead,"
the grey goose said.
Snip, snip, snip.

The tiny woman wanted a coat.

"Where will I get a needle?"

"Have one of mine,"
said the porcupine.
Sharp, sharp, sharp.

The tiny woman wanted a coat.

"Where will I get some thread?"

"My mane, of course,"
said the friendly horse.
Stitch, stitch, stitch.

The tiny woman wanted a coat.

"Where will I get some buttons?"

"Take some of our seeds,"
said the wild wet weeds.
One, two, *three.*

The tiny woman put on her coat
and went out into the storm.

She stayed as snug
as a bug in a rug,
with her coat to keep her warm.

This edition first published in 2021 by Gecko Press
PO Box 9335, Wellington 6141, New Zealand
info@geckopress.com

Text © Joy Cowley 1987
Illustrations © Giselle Clarkson 2021
Edition © Gecko Press 2021

Distributed in the United States and Canada by Lerner Publishing Group, lernerbooks.com
Distributed in the United Kingdom by Bounce Sales and Marketing, bouncemarketing.co.uk
Distributed in Australia and New Zealand by Walker Books Australia, walkerbooks.com.au

The author and publisher thank Wendy Pye Publishing Ltd for permission to reproduce the text.

Gecko Press acknowledges the generous support of Creative New Zealand

creative *nz*
ARTS COUNCIL OF NEW ZEALAND TOI AOTEAROA

Design and typesetting by Vida Kelly
Printed in China by Everbest Printing Co. Ltd,
an accredited ISO 14001 & FSC-certified printer

ISBN hardback 978-1-776573-42-4
Ebook available

For more curiously good books, visit geckopress.com